LIKE COCOI

A Short Story
By Tochukwu Chike Muonagolu

oo oo oo ꧁꧂ oo oo oo

The sun was low in the sky as a cool breeze swept gently across the land, throwing dust everywhere. It was just a few minutes past seven in the evening, and all over the town of Oshodi, people rounded off their businesses in the joy of retiring home. In Oshodi, the buildings, which were all old and shabby, leaned close to each other in crooked rows and columns, and several narrow roads cut through them, linking the small town with other parts of Lagos. But there was really no place in Lagos like Oshodi. The town was a chaotic place that constantly buzzed with vehicles and people from all walks of life.

In Oshodi, there was a famous motor park beside one of the pedestrian bridges that ran over the Oshodi highway. It was a big motor park with a bustling market, a popular destination for buses travelling into the city of Lagos. In front of the park's main entrance, just around the corner where men from the North sold cigarettes and candies, a large signpost read: Welcome to Oshodi City Park.

That evening, a passenger lorry stood in front of the park's main entrance. At the back of the lorry, the phrase "BACK TO SENDER" was boldly printed for those with an evil eye. The man who drove the lorry had dropped off some passengers at the motor park earlier that day and was now leaving with a new set of passengers. Meanwhile, the traders at the motor park, who sold everything from vehicle parts to books and pencils, were stowing and locking up their stores. As they did so, their voices mingled with the music that blared from several audio systems. Also, the motor park's kingpin, a famous woman who went by the name Mama Oshodi, had instructed her men to lock all the gates leading to the motor park to prevent motorists from driving in. After her men had locked the gates, they retired to leisure activities and their places of rest. It was this way every evening with Mama Oshodi and her men and the traders who sold at the motor park.

Everyone knew who Mama Oshodi was. She was something along the lines of a local champion at the motor park. Her real name was Eniola. But only a few of her men knew her by that name, not to mention the traders at the motor park. She had a sturdy physique and was neither tall nor short. Except for her breasts, which stuck out a little, and her high-pitched voice, nothing suggested that she was a woman in her late forties. She kept her hair short and walked around in oversized shirts and jeans. The thirty-something man gang she controlled functioned in a loosely organized way. The gang comprised young men between the ages of sixteen and thirty, and these young men helped her run the motor park. Their duties mainly involved assisting her in collecting the park's entrance fee from motorists, and ensuring that they parked their vehicles in the right places to avoid congestion. For this work, Mama Oshodi let the men keep some of the money. Most of her men, if not all of them, revered her to a great extent.

Amongst Mama Oshodi's men, was a young man named, Chibuzo, an Igbo name that means *God is the way*. But everyone, including his parents, called him Uzo for short. He was about six feet tall and heavy-looking, and his skin was as black as coal. He looked a lot like his mother and very little like his father, who was short and yellow like papaya. That evening, Uzo retired with members of his unit, a small section of Mama Oshodi's gang, to a popular roadside restaurant managed by a middle-aged woman known as Mama Bisi. Bisi was her daughter's name, of course; no one knew her actual name. To the novice, Mama Bisi's place was just a typical Buka that sold street food. But the people who visited there frequently knew the extra goodies Mama Bisi provided. Now, Uzo had almost finished smoking his fourth roll of Ibo, the street name for marijuana, but he still could not smother the anger and restlessness in him. On the bench in front of him sat two big bowls of Amala and Ewedu. Kehinde, his closest friend, sat beside him on his left side, while Ajayi, Tunde and Dada—who was also known as Idowu, sat opposite him. These were the members of Uzo's unit. And Ajayi, the most intelligent of them, was their leader.

Everyone was in high spirits that evening except for Uzo. He had no appetite for the food in front of him, and he kept adjusting himself on the bench he was sitting on as if someone were poking his buttocks with the tip of a nail. It was not hard, however, to see the reason for his discomfort because it was clearly written all over him. There was a nasty bruise on the left side of his face, and the eyelid there was so swollen he could barely open his eye. At the corner of his upper lip was a deep cut that made it difficult for him to close his lips, and his football jersey was torn along its rib and length. Most of the people he had come across since the incident occurred that afternoon did not bother to ask him what had happened. They just told him, "Pẹlẹ" *Sorry,* or made consoling remarks along the lines of, "Don't worry, it shall be well."

So now, Uzo sat there, smoking and worrying about how to avoid his mother when he gets home. When his friends suggested he come with them to the house party that was happening later that night at the apartment of a young man known as Jay-B, he angrily declined. He thought it was stupid of them to ask him to come to a party when he looked like a person that had just been run over by a car. Moreover, he did not like Jay-B. His actual name was Jide Bankole, and his father, Chief Bankole, was a local politician and a wealthy landlord in Oshodi. He was familiar with those parties Jay-B threw on the weekends, and he knew it would be good for him to avoid it now. Showing up there would only make him a laughing stock. Besides, Akani, the girl he liked very much would most likely be there, and this was not how he should appear looking in front of her. He stood up and walked out of the restaurant without saying goodbye to anyone. The one-bedroom flat he shared with his parents was not far away.

Outside, the sky had turned completely dark, and under the few stars that shinned brightly, Uzo headed down the dusty road that led to Balogun street where his parents' flat stood. In front of him, the dusty road curved like a carpet viper, and noisy vehicles rushed up and down, honking loudly at themselves. There were many yellow Danfo buses clumped together in a long yellow line along both sides of the road, and a dirty smell from the canal that ran along the road's concrete pavement filled the air. People walked up and down the pavement, brushing past themselves as they hurried to their destinations. But Uzo walked at a slow pace, as if all the time in the world belonged to him, and though this made some of the people behind him angry, he did not care. He was thinking hard of a suitable explanation to give his mother for his tattered jersey and the bruises on his face. It would be difficult to make her believe something other than the truth because this was not the first time he was coming home looking this way. What happened at the motor park that day had been happening quite often recently, and he had always had to come up with an excuse for his bruises and ruffled look. The last time it happened, which was only a few weeks ago, his mother gave him a stern warning not to come home looking like a homeless dog again. He thought of going to the party that his friends had invited him to so that he could avoid his mother for a while, but Akani would be there, and he did not want her to see him this way. Her full name was Akani Alakija, and she was a lean beauty with a skin as black as his. But that was all they had in common—the skin colour. They barely spoke to each other, and whenever he tried, he always found himself stuttering and saying rubbish: things that did not make any sense and things that did not whet her appetite. He could always tell from her reaction, the way she would roll her eyes and curve her lips into a mocking smile. Except for his name, she knew nothing about him. But he knew everything about her. That her father was a barrister and the owner of a successful law firm, and that she was the only child of her mother whom she lost in a road accident when she was only twelve years old. Of course, he knew that part of her because she always narrated the tragic event to her friends and anyone that cared to listen in an effortless way, as though none of it really concerned her. Whenever she recalled the events of that awful day, she would shrug her shoulders and explain that the thin scar on her left temple was an outcome of the accident. He thought the scar made her look even more beautiful, but he had not yet found the courage to tell her that.

"Brother Uzo, How far? You don return? You buy anytin for us?" It was Damilola, their neighbour's six-year-old son. He had noticed Uzo walking into the yard from the corner of the balcony where he was playing and was greeting him with a wide smile on his face.

"Ta! Comot for my face Joor!" Uzo replied, irritated by the boy's greetings. "I resemble your papa?" He added. "Abeg, make you mind how you dey shout my name for this compound O. I no be your mate."

Uzo sucked his teeth, then took off his worn-out rubber slippers and held them in his hands. "Dis world sef," He muttered angrily to himself as he went into the room he shared with his parents. "Pikin wey dey just born yesterday no dey fear person face again."

Inside the room, Uzo's mother sat next to a cooking stove. She was patiently removing stones and black ants from a large tray of uncooked beans while humming to the gospel song playing from her old cassette player. The only light in the living room came from the dim kerosene lantern that sat on the dining table, but Uzo could easily make out the features on his mother's face and knew she would, likewise, not have a hard time noticing that there was something off about his appearance. He shut the door quietly behind him and waited.

"Ah, Uzo," She called. Then a worried expression crept over her face. "Kedu ihe mere gi?" She asked. What happened to you?

"Mama, good evening." Uzo replied, his words barely audible. He was avoiding her gaze, and he pondered how to get to the bedroom door across the room without having to confront her.

"Yes, nnoo, mana gini mere i jiri di otu a?" You are welcome, but why do you look this way? She said to him, her voice rising with alarm.

"Eh?" Uzo replied, pretending not to understand the Igbo his mother was speaking.

"Na me you dey ask eh? You dey craze?" His mother said, changing the tone in her voice. "I say why you be like person wey panel beater knack!"

"Nobody beat me, mama." Uzo muttered, adjusting his t-shirt. "Na just one small crisis wey catch me for road today."

Believing he had said enough and cautiously avoiding his angry and bewildered mother, he dashed across the room, went into the bedroom and banged the door close. Outside the room, his mother threatened and shouted at him to come back out and explain himself, but he ignored her.

The bedroom, which was where Uzo's entire family slept in, was a very small one. It had just one window for ventilation, and the window had a green mosquito net built into its sliding sash and grey metal bars. At the centre of the white concrete ceiling above the room, hung an incandescent light bulb that dropped down to provide illumination. The four walls of the bedroom were painted teal blue, like the ocean at the Lagos bar beach. And on the back wall, hung a wedding picture of Uzo's parents—his mother smiling broadly in it as she towered several inches over his father. On the dot patterned concrete floor, were two foam mattresses for sleeping: one for Uzo, and the larger one for his parents.

Uzo had known this room all his life, although his mother once told him that they moved into the flat from Onitsha, a small town in Anambra, when he was barely two years old. He could not remember much about then, except he had felt quite lonely being the only child of his parents. He used to cry and demand that his mother give birth to another child, and a boy to be precise, so that he could have a partner to play with. But when his mother eventually gave birth to another child, he was disappointed because it was a girl. His father, however, had named her Obiageli, which means, the one who came to eat. He had promised her in an ecstatic joy the first day he met her that he would spoil her with all the luxury money could buy. But Uzo's father knew he was not wealthy enough to keep that promise. He only believed that saying such things would make the newborn child bring some luck to his business, because according to his tradition, babies had not yet forgotten the gates to the spirit world.

Unlike Uzo, Obiageli was a replica of his father. Her skin was as yellow as the sun, and her eyes were big and brown. She was a beautiful baby, and everyone was always quick to assert it. She cried a lot the first few weeks after she came home from the hospital. Some nights, when it rained and she cried, her wails would pierce the sounds of angry waters splashing against their zinc roof, so much so that sometimes the rain would stop just to console her. Later, when she started to take her first steps, unsteady as she was, Uzo would lead her gently and patiently to their balcony and point out things to her.

"Dat one is a motor."

"Say, Maangoo Treee."

"You see dat Okada? Na Uncle Musa own." Uzo would say, often asking her to repeat after him.

Obiageli always watched him eager to do everything he did. It made Uzo laugh sometimes, but he was happy. He loved her, more than words can describe, and he felt a strong sense of duty to protect her. So, when she died three years later after falling ill with malaria and typhoid because that was what they assumed she had, he blamed himself for her demise. But that was many years ago. Now, Uzo laid on his mattress in the tiny bedroom, listening to the gentle voice of King Sunny Ade coming from a record player outside the building. He found the pleasant melody of the song relaxing, and it made him want to sing along. But he did not know the lyrics of the song that well. Only the first two lines which he sang pensively as he stared at the concrete ceiling above him.

Ori mi ye o, jaaaa ja funmi.

Eda mí ye o, jaaaa ja funmi.

He sang with a voice filled with sadness.

Every now and then, he felt the stinging pain from his bruises. To ease the pain, he dipped his jersey into the bucket of water in the bedroom and pressed the cloth gently against his face. When the music died, the memory of the fight that occurred at the motor park that afternoon crawled back into his mind, and arranged itself in sequence like soldiers falling in line. He felt anger rising in him again as he wondered why Kehinde and the rest of his mates had not come to his rescue. Defending themselves was their unwritten law, something they did to reinforce their sense of brotherhood, an instinct embedded deep within them. But Ajayi had warned him about that man, and he had chosen not to listen. He had measured the stubby man himself, and did not think he was going to be that much of a problem.

It was only a few minutes past one that afternoon when the man drove his old Volkswagen bus to the gate where Uzo and his friends were stationed, blaring his horns loud as if to alert everyone of his long-awaited arrival. When Kehinde noticed him, he quickly placed a handmade tyre-killer in front of the bus, thus forcing it to come to a halt. That was the tactic they used to prevent drivers who did not want to pay the entrance fee from escaping them. It was Uzo's turn to collect the fees so he approached the bus. He observed the bus closely and assumed the driver must be coming from one of the neighbouring states due to the Yoruba slogans impressed all over the body of his vehicle. He thought the driver looked familiar, but he could not recall any encounter he might have had with him. He observed the man at the front passenger seat, and the woman who sat beside him with a child suckling at her breast. When Uzo caught the driver's eye, the man's face broke into a wide smile that revealed his bone-white teeth and stretched the deep tribal marks that ran up his cheeks like old wounds from the clawing of a wild beast. From of the corner of his mouth, hung an over chewed chewing stick. He greeted Uzo, and his smile turned into a wicked grin. Uzo returned his greetings but gave no room for light conversations. Then, with a stern look on his face, Uzo told the driver that the entrance fee would be three hundred Naira and nothing less. The man stared at him for a few seconds, then burst into a laughter that exposed his full teeth and the dark gums in his mouth. He laughed so hard that his chest heaved and tears formed at the corners of his eyes. Feeling insulted, Uzo's face tightened and deep lines formed in his brow.

"Bros, you no know who I be?" The driver asked as he tried to catch his breath that reeked of tobacco. "Ah, you think say I be JJC for Lagos, abi?"

"Oga, na three hundred everybody dey pay to enter Park. If you no wan bring money, abeg clear comot for road make oder people see space enter." Uzo replied, throwing his arms away to tell the man he could go to hell.

The driver laughed again, but not as much this time. Then, adjusting the chewing stick in his mouth, he said to Uzo, "Bros, no be say I no wan pay to enter Park. I go pay. But no be three hundred wey I go pay."

"See," He added, pulling out some worn-out banknotes from his breast pocket. "Na only one hundred Naira remain for my body. Abeg, collect am make I dey go. I no get time to waste." He said to Uzo.

"For where! I no fit!" Uzo retorted angrily "If you no get three hundred for hand, carry dis your nonsense motor comot for my face joor!" To show the man he meant business, he feigned searching the ground for an object to strike the bus with.

The man grinned, then dug into the pockets of his trousers and pulled out a Twenty Naira note, and a Ten Naira note. Then, he arranged all the banknotes neatly and in ascending order and held them out in his hand for Uzo to collect.

"Oya, na everything I get be dis." He said with a solemn look on his face. "Open de gate, make I pass."

Feeling frustrated, Uzo nearly spat at the man. He thought the money he would gain from the One Hundred and Thirty Naira was too small. He did the calculation in his mind. If he gave fifty Naira to Mama Oshodi, and thirty percent of the remaining amount to Ajayi, as their custom demanded, he would be left with just about fifty-five Naira only. A violent storm rose in his chest at the thought of this.

"You be bastard!" He blurted out, stretching out his palm and hand towards the driver, his temper flaring like a wild flame. But the man would not be intimidated. He stepped down from his bus, and staring into Uzo's eyes, dared him to call him a bastard one more time. The baby that had been suckling at its mother's breast began to cry. And when Kehinde, Dada and Tunde, noticed the tension building up between Uzo and the man, they ran towards them to ease things up.

Uzo and the driver were still sizing up themselves when Ajayi arrived a few minutes later. A small crowd had gathered around the two men, and amongst them were some passengers who had disembarked from the man's bus to help resolve the quarrel. Ajayi knew the man. The two were acquainted.

"Kilode, wetin happen?" He asked Uzo as he pulled him aside and away from the crowd. Uzo's feet were unsteady, and he fumed like a kettle on a stove. He made an attempt to return to his face-off with the man, but Ajayi restrained him.

"Farabalè!" Calm down! Ajayi said, forcing Uzo to stand still and explain what had happened. Uzo narrated his experience with the man. But then, he claimed that during the face-off, the man had referred to him as Inyamuri, a tribalistic slur for a person of Igbo descent. Ajayi understood Uzo's anger, but he wanted him to see things from a different perspective so that he could let what the man had said go away. He told him that the driver was not a bad man. He visited the bus park frequently and was even well acquainted with some of their friends in Oshodi. Besides, the man used to be in the military, and he knows quite a few people there. It would be wise, he explained, to maintain a good relationship with the man.

"Just collect de money. E no too small like dat sef." Ajayi told him.

But Uzo would not listen. He was too offended by what the man had called him. He fought his way out of Ajayi's arms and charged towards the man, who had been beckoning him to come forward and do his worst. Seeing as Uzo charged at him, the man armed himself with a rock and took a fighting stance. There was an upheaval in the small crowd that had gathered around. Some of the people in the crowd moved in front of the man to prevent Uzo from getting to him, but Uzo had calculated his move and was quick. He ducked under their arms and grabbed the man around his left thigh. The rock fell. Quickly, Uzo tightened his grip and yanked the man around, hoping to throw him down and get over with the fight. But the man was heavier than he thought, and his right leg stood firmly on the ground. They struggled that way until the man managed to wrap his arms around Uzo's waist. Then, when he felt more secure in his balance, he grabbed Uzo's neck with his right arm, pulled his head under his armpit, and locked it there. Then using his right hand again, he grabbed Uzo along the waistline of his trousers, lifted him into the air, swung around and knocked him down with a heavy thud. It was over then, but the man was not done. Pinning Uzo to the ground like a cat to a mouse, he dealt his face many blows until his mouth became filled with the metallic taste of blood. Behind them, the crowd only clamoured for the man to have mercy on the boy.

Now, Uzo sighed, letting out a long deep breath. The night had become serene, only disturbed by the sounds of singing crickets and toads. He dug into his pocket, took out the One hundred and Thirty Naira and studied each banknote as though they were something unfamiliar. The driver had thrown it at him before walking back to his bus, and Ajayi had told him to keep everything. He was glad, but he was not sure if the money was worth the beating. He turned around on the mattress he was lying on to ease the pain on his back. He was just about falling asleep when the bedroom door swung open, and his father staggered in, the stench of tobacco and beer following strongly behind him. He said something to Uzo, but his words were too slurred and incoherent for Uzo to figure out what he wanted. Uzo ignored him, and soon they were both stretched out on their mattresses, snoring away.

∾⚬⚬⚬⚬⚬∾

Uzo's father's name was Uche Ejiofor. He was a taxi driver, but he found the title demeaning. Chauffeur sounded more pleasing to him, even though what he did was not any different from what the taxi drivers in Lagos did for a living. He drove a yellow 95 Volkswagen Golf 3 around the city of Lagos, picking passengers and dropping them at their various destinations. It was a job life exerted on him, and it showed in his bearing. But it had not always been so. His story goes back to the days when he used to drive passengers in those rickety lorries with large wooden boots around the town of Onitsha. He was only sixteen then, but he had hopes and dreams big enough to fill the ocean. At the age of twenty-one, he started driving long distances, transporting traders from Onitsha to the big cities in the western part of the country. He drove up to the North sometimes, but only as far as Lafia and Jos. It was on his return from one of those long-distance trips that he met Chinelo and fell in love. She was two years older than him and taller too, but that did not discourage him. He would visit her at her mother's shed at the Onitsha Main Market to confess his love for her, and she would give him bananas and peanuts to eat. He used to tell her some of his dreams: how he wanted to start his own transportation company someday and his plans to travel the world when he becomes rich. Chinelo developed an affection for him because she found it amusing that a man like him, a man from her side of the planet, would be dreaming of travelling the world. She was a pragmatic kind of person. Buying and selling, and calculating her profits and losses were what she knew best. Travelling the world, however, she thought, was the kind of thing you only saw in the movies or read in books or heard musicians sing about on the radio.

She did not believe he would ever travel the world, and she teased him every time he mentioned it to her.

"Ọ bụ obere ụkwụ gi ị ga-eji gaa London na Paris?" Is it those short legs you are going to use to go to London and Paris? She would say to him, laughing and rubbing her palms in that manner that looked like she was removing dirt from them.

But the two were in love. Some evenings, after she had taken permission from her mother, he would drive her in his lorry until they reached the bank of the River Niger, and there they would sit and watch the fishermen paddle their colourful canoes back to shore under the setting sun. Whenever a canoe arrived at the sandy shore, fish sellers would flock around it like ants attacking sugary food. They would haggle and tussle with the fishermen over the cost of their fishes, and when they finally left, the canoe would be empty of all the fishes the fishermen had caught. Sometimes, Uche and Chinelo would buy peppery fried fish wrapped in old newspapers from the fish sellers at the river bank and eat together at the boot of his lorry while grooving to the sounds of Apostles of Aba and Billy Ocean. They courted that way for three years before getting married at a small catholic church on Oguta road in Onitsha. There had been no proposal. Only discussions, visits and lots of planning. A year after they got married, they had Uzo. And while Uche continued to drive his lorry, Chinelo and the child lived with Uche's parents in a small apartment in Onitsha. Later, when one of Uche's cousins offered him a job that involved driving a Lebanese expatriate who was working with an oil company in Lagos, Uche decided to give the job a try. The job paid considerably well and was less stressful than driving a lorry all over the country, so he sold his lorry soon after he started the job, bought a one-bedroom flat on Balogun street in Oshodi, and moved his family there. Uzo was barely two then.

When they first moved to Lagos, Chinelo complained a lot about how noisy the city was and how it robbed her of her privacy. She wanted to go back to Onitsha, but Uche thought they needed the change of air. Besides, he said to her once as she complained, Lagos is like a Coconut fruit. It is only those who break it that can drink its water. But she kept complaining, so he bought her a partially furnished lock-up store on Church Street, which was a walking distance from their one-bedroom flat, and stocked it with provisions so that she could trade to keep herself busy. Later, when Chinelo gave birth to Obiageli, Uche repainted their flat and refurnished the living room. He was happy because life had been kind to him, and the future seemed bright. But when Obiageli died three years later, he became depressed and turned to alcohol for relief. It took him nearly two years to pull himself out of the mess he became: after his Lebanese boss had threatened to relieve him of his duty, and after Chinelo had confided in a neighbour who advised her to take her husband to a prophet in Mushin for prayers and exorcism. Surprisingly, Uche stopped drinking after the prophet prayed over him. But Chinelo knew it was the shame that came with the public confession and rejection of alcohol, a mortification the prophet had forced him to do, that made him quit his behaviour.

Uche drove the Lebanese for ten years, until the oil company he worked for suddenly terminated his contract, and the man left the country. He was only in his mid-thirties then when he stopped driving the Lebanese, but being jobless and having to depend on his wife made him feel like a failure. He had saved very little from the money he earned while driving the Lebanese, so there was nothing for him to fall back on. Nothing to start a business or a trade, and nothing to buy even another lorry. Uzo dropped out of secondary school because there was no money to pay his fees, and their family became the joke of the neighbourhood. Everyone gossiped behind them, and friends, or rather people they thought were their friends, stopped visiting. Their little world had crumbled, and the rubbles fell on Uche's head. And though he could have found another driving job to keep his family afloat, he chose not to do so. He had the feeling life had packed all her belongings and walked out of his door for good, a feeling of despair even he could not understand.

When Uche's mother died a few months later, he started drinking again. Alcohol and rage, then the feeling of despair and alcohol again. It became a cycle that entrapped him. Sometimes, he would weep at night and Chinelo would take him into her arms and console him. She did not think their situation was that bad. As long as they were all alive and healthy and together, there was hope. But Uche could not see things that way. It was as if he had broken himself while trying to break the coconut fruit. Uzo felt sorry for his father, but his weakness and selfishness repulsed him. So, for a long time, he dug a deep trench between he and his father, and guarded it with a cold attitude. He only started being a little sentimental towards him, when at the age of fifteen, he came home one afternoon and found his father trying to end his life. He was standing on the kitchen stool, a blue polypropylene rope tied around his neck and a bottle of Ogogoro on the floor. When Uzo saw the distant look in his father's eyes and it dawned on him what he was trying to do, a fear that took weeks to fade away seized him, and he screamed so much that their neighbours came running to their flat. They prevented the suicide from happening, and when Chinelo returned from her store that evening, the neighbours told her what had happened. She wept as expected, but she was quick to gather herself back together. She did not believe getting back the man she fell in love with was a task beyond her control. So the next day, she went all the way to Badagry, a town located on the outskirts of Lagos, to see an old friend of theirs, one Bamidele who was a used-car dealer. After Chinelo told Bamidele about Uche's condition and pleaded for assistance, the man decided to sell them a Volkswagen golf 3 at a price that was less than half the purchasing cost, but on the condition that Uche would register the car as a city taxi. Uche did as Bamidele advised, but he never recovered from his alcohol addiction. The depth of that pit was already too deep for him to climb back out.

Uzo woke up to a pale morning sky and a sun red with glory. The atmosphere in the town of Oshodi was lazy and relaxed, a tranquility that would, of course, cease to exist once all those lorries and buses filled with noisy commuters and traders begin their daily journeys in and out of the small town. When Uzo got to the motor park, he bought a breakfast of bread and beans porridge from Mama Bisi, then settled down beside a rusty brown gate to eat. Not too far from him, a skinny brown dog walked about, sniffing the ground as though it were looking for something it had misplaced. A week had passed since Uzo fought with the man, and his bruises had formed a hard grey crust that covered the soft flesh beneath his skin. His eyes were no longer swollen, and his jawbones appeared to be symmetrical again. Uzo was so focused on his meal that he failed to notice Kehinde approaching him, a tall and lean figure with a short dusty brown hair that gleamed under the sun. Kehinde had his own breakfast wrapped in a small plastic bag and was walking in hurried steps.

"Uzo!" He called.

Uzo looked up to see who it was.

"Ah, Kehinde, na you," he replied, chewing the food in his mouth. "Guy, how far na?" he added as he chewed some more.

Kehinde acknowledged Uzo's greetings, then sucked his teeth in that quick manner that showed excitement. Then, sitting next to Uzo, he untied the plastic bag and set a loaf of bread and two balls of Akara in between his legs.

"Bros, you no go believe wetin happen for night yesterday," he said, opening the loaf of bread with his hand and placing the balls of Akara in-between the bread.

"Wetin happen?" Uzo asked. Then looking up at Kehinde from the corner of his eye, he added, "Dis one wey just dey shine teeth for Monday morning, I know say na woman wey jam you."

"Ode, no be woman," Kehinde replied.

"So wetin e come be?"

Kehinde grinned and shook his head excitedly. "You know dat my mama cousin wey I tell you dey live for Turkey?"

"Yes, wetin do am?" Uzo asked.

"She come back yesterday." Kehinde replied, grinning.

Uzo looked at his friend's face to understand where he was going with the discussion, how the news of the return of his mother's cousin concerned him and his work at the motor park.

"So na dis tin you wan tell me?" Uzo finally said.

"You sef! You no understand?" Kehinde replied. "You suppose to know say person wey just come back from abroad gats to hold plenty money!" "See," he continued, tapping Uzo on his shoulder, "As we dey here dey talk, my mama don already enter early morning bus to go see am for Togo where she dey."

Uzo sucked his teeth dismissively. "So na for Togo she dey. If you tell me say she dey your Mama house, I for see small sense for dis your talk." "Abeg free me joor," he added, shrugging Kehinde's hand away from him. "De only tin wey dey my mind now na de money I go collect today."

Kehinde laughed out loud. "So you never tire for dis job wey we dey do here so?" "Come make I ask you," he added, leaning close to Uzo. "You get plans for your life?"

"Plans…for my life" Uzo asked with a confused expression on his face. "Which kin question be dat? Wetin pass de work wey we dey do here?"

"You see yourself. Na poor man mentality dey worry you." Kehinde said. "You no know say as we dey here so, we suppose to dey tink big, dey tink outside dis yeye park." "Okay come, make I ask you anoda question," Kehinde continued, adjusting himself on the bench, "Dat fine girl, Akani, wey you like, you don ask yourself why she no dey give you face?"

"Abeg, no bring Akani inside dis talk. If you no get real talk for your mouth, just keep am shut make I dey go." Uzo replied, a bit angry at his friend.

Kehinde chuckled, and his shoulders heaved spasmodically. When he calmed down, he spoke in a more serious tone.

"See, de tin I want say be dis. Dat my mama cousin get plenty money, and her money no be small money at all. In fact, when my mama comot for house dis morning, she carry three bags for hand becus de woman talk say she bring plenty tins for us. And me, I dey suspect money join de tins wey she carry come." Then he paused and looked over his shoulders to see if there was anyone close enough to hear what he was saying. At a distance, a young woman was scrubbing her child in a bucket filled with soapy water, and the skinny brown dog was sitting quietly, nibbling on something it had picked up from a garbage bin. Kehinde leaned closer to Uzo and carried on.

"But you know de part wey dey sweet me about de whole tin? Dat my mama cousin love me soté she dey always call my mama to ask am if I fit come join her for de business wey she dey do for Turkey. So, as my mama don go her place now, she wan tell her make she carry me go back."

Uzo's lips curved slightly and he smiled. "So you dey tell me say dem dey make plans for you to comot dis country?" He asked with a raised eyebrow.

"You talk am!" Kehinde confirmed, bursting into laughter. "In fact, as you see me so, I don already become Oyinbo!"

Uzo laughed, and the two clasped their hands in an emotional handshake. It was good to hear that his friend would soon be on his way out of the country for a better life overseas. And though he found it hard to imagine Kehinde in the land of the white man, because after all, he was just an Agbero like him, the news brought him a feeling of hope; that anything might actually be possible, that maybe, he too might one day leave the dirty motor park to explore other opportunities in life. He could start an importation business, make lots of money, buy a nice car, marry Akani, and raise beautiful children with her. Maybe, if he worked hard and smart enough, he could finally break that coconut fruit. He was lost in his thoughts when Kehinde suddenly pulled him up from the bench and invited him to dance to the loud music playing from the stereo system at a nearby store. The sound of the drums and the sweet melody of the saxophone thrilled the two young men, and they danced under the morning sun, moving their bodies unreservedly to the rhythm of the beat. When the music stopped, they walked, tired and exhausted, to the main gate of the motor park where Ajayi stood waiting for them.

The sun burned their skin as they listened to Ajayi who stood akimbo, delivering instructions in a loud and confident voice. His face was void of expression as he reminded the men about their duties and daily tasks. Today, he wanted Dada and Tunde to watch the main gate, while Uzo and Kehinde covered the leaks. There were reports that truck pushers had been sneaking in through broken fences to avoid paying the motor park's entrance fee, so Uzo and Kehinde would keep an eye out for them. When Ajayi finished his speech, he led Uzo and Kehinde to a partially collapsed wall that was not too far from the main gate.

"You see am?" Ajayi said, pointing out the wall to them. "Na from here many of dem dey come in from."

There were deep cracks etched all over on the wall, and close to the corner where the wall joined another wall, a large hole the shape of a man's fist gaped openly at them. Beneath the hole, rocks and debris littered the crumbling earth and overgrown bushes. Again, Ajayi instructed the two men to stay and watch, and to make sure they apprehend anyone trying to come in or leave through the wall. After Uzo and Kehinde assured him that they would do as he had instructed, he turned and marched away. Feeling a bit apathetic, the two young men settled down on a concrete slab and watched the wall.

They sat there on the slab for two hours, bored and itchy from the bites of tiny mosquitoes and black flies. It was already noon, and no one had showed up yet at the fence. But just when they had given up hope and were about to leave the vicinity, they noticed movements on the other side of the wall. Then, suddenly feeling excited at the thought that they might have found an offender, they sat back and watched quietly.

"Shhh! No talk anytin!" Uzo whispered to Kehinde. He wanted whoever it was to make it well through the wall before confronting them. As they watched in silence, they saw the wooden frame of a cart appear through the hole, followed by two big wheels. The person handling the cart seemed to be having a hard time maneuvering through the rocks and debris because they kept moving back and forth. But when the person responsible for the movements finally became visible through the hole, Uzo leaned forward to get a closer look. It was a young man with a gaunt frame, and his box-shaped head bobbed back and forth as he pushed and pulled awkwardly at the dilapidated cart. He was wearing a grease-stained t-shirt and an oversized three-quarter jean, and in his cart was a tall stack of neatly arranged cartons, each one meticulously placed against the other to provide mutual support. Every now and then, Uzo and Kehinde lost sight of the young man because he kept disappearing behind the tall stack of cartons only to reappear from a different side. When the young man eventually made it through the hole, he parked his cart next to the fence so that he could stretch his arms. But he could barely do any stretching because he kept looking over his shoulders to see if anyone was watching him. When he noticed Uzo and Kehinde, he picked up the yoke of the cart and began pushing in the opposite direction. Uzo and Kehinde sprang to their feet and followed him.

"Hey! Where you dey go?!" Uzo called.

"Stop dere!" Kehinde added.

They were running to catch up with the young man who was now pushing harder against his cart, ignoring their calls and acting as if he was oblivious to them. But Uzo and Kehinde soon reached him, and he had no choice but to face them.

"You no dey hear? Na where you tink say you dey go?" Uzo asked the young man, seizing him by the bottom hem of his t-shirt. Kehinde stood in front of his cart, glaring.

"Ah-ah, wetin happen?" The young man stammered with a worried look on his face.

"You dey craze!" Kehinde scolded. No be you wey just comot from dat fence?"

The young man's instinct was to resist and deny the accusation, but he thought closely about the situation and decided he might have a better chance of getting through if he just admitted his offence. He began to plead.

"My broda, abeg, make you no vex," the young man pleaded, tilting his head to one side. "I jus say make I use dis road today because everywhere don block finish."

"Sharap!" Uzo retorted. "Dis place be like road for your eyes?" He was not in the mood to listen to any pleas, and neither was Kehinde. The two had not made a single naira since morning, and they were worried about being able to afford at least a drink for lunch.

"Oya, give us one hundred naira make you go!" Uzo demanded nonchalantly, as if he was doing the young man a favour by only asking for that much.

But the young man let out a cry of dismay and pulled out his pockets to show Uzo and Kehinde that he had nothing to give. "I never even chop anytin since yesterday." He cried, hoping to invoke their sympathy. "Na de small money my Oga wan pay me for dis cartons wey I carry wey I wan take buy food chop."

"Oloshi Oloriburuku!" Wretched fool! Kehinde mocked the young man with disgust. "Na your papa own dis park, abi?" "Oh, you no know say people dey pay gate fee before dem dey enter here?"

"Ah! Me I no know O!" The young man swore, raising his hands to the sky as if to demonstrate the extent of his ignorance. "If to say I know, I for tell de people wey give me dis carton make dem also give me—"

"E don do!" Uzo interrupted the young man. He did not have the patience to listen to his excuses. "Okay, if you get fifty Naira for your hand, give us. We fit manage dat one." He demanded in a harsh tone that betrayed his desperation.

But the young man fell on his knees and pleaded. "Abeg, abeg I no get money. I not get at all."

"So wetin you fit give us na?" Kehinde asked angrily.

"My broda, I no fit lie for you." The young man replied, touching the earth and his tongue with his fingers, and raising his hand up to the sky. "If I get money, I for don give you."

Uzo thought of letting the young man go, but his demons reminded him of the two hours he had spent under the sun waiting for someone to show up. So, he decided that the young man ought to be taught a lesson for trying to sneak in through the wall. Feeling no pity for the young man any longer, he grabbed the yoke of his cart and began pulling backwards in an attempt to seize the equipment. When the young man sensed what was about to happen, he stood up and ran to Uzo.

"For where! You no fit take am!" The young man protested as he struggled to take back control of the cart, which was his only source of livelihood. "Ję ki n ku kuku ku!" Let me die instead! He shouted, drawing the attention of passersby and traders.

Kehinde moved in quickly to assist his friend. He pulled the young man away from Uzo and locked his arms in a tight grip to prevent him from returning to his cart. But it was difficult to hold the man down because he had become frantic and violent and was raving as though a bolt had suddenly gone loose in his head. He slipped out of Kehinde's grip like a catfish and dashed towards Uzo who had begun pushing the cart towards the main gate.

"Comot dere joor!" The truck pusher exclaimed, running into Uzo with the force of his entire body and knocking him away from the cart.

Uzo staggered only to regain his balance before falling to the ground. "Ah," he gaped, lost for words and taken aback by the young man's strength. He thought of retaliating with a more vicious attack but decided to enlighten the man a bit, to let him know who he and Kehinde worked for and the power they held at the motor park, that they were obliged to seize his cart because he had trespassed on their territory. But when he spoke, his words were like a foreign language in the ears of the young man who just kept swinging his arms, warning both of them not to come near him or his cart. Uzo felt a strong urge to thrash the young man, but he knew he had to save his energy for the other brawls he would definitely get into later in the afternoon. He thought there was no use wasting his energy on someone so miserable, someone whose pockets were as dry as an abandoned well. Using his hand and facial gestures to communicate, he instructed Kehinde to restrain the young man again so that he could move the cart away. Kehinde nodded and moved cautiously towards him. But there was something different about the young man that terrified Kehinde now, and it was not the ferocity with which he swung his arms. It had to do with his determination, the fearless look in his eyes that said he was ready to risk everything because he had nothing to lose.

A small crowd soon gathered, and the few men who stepped forward to settle the quarrel withdrew as soon as they discovered it involved Mama Oshodi's men. But some people spoke in hushed tones, condemning Uzo and Kehinde for trying to rob the poor young man off his only possession. And a woman who was so displeased by the scene walked away from it quietly. Now, Kehinde held the young man's face against the ground and planted his knees firmly on his upper spine to restrict his movements, while Uzo pushed the cart hurriedly and with great effort towards the main gate. He was not comfortable with the crowd because it made him feel naked, and it made the situation seem out of control. He tried focusing his mind on getting the cart to the main gate, where he knew he would receive the full support of Ajayi and the other men, but the overburdened cart was too cumbersome to move, and his arms were starting to ache. In a bid to reduce the weight, he paused and began unloading the cart.

"No touch am O! You go pay for am O!" The young man warned Uzo, yelling at the top of his lungs. But Uzo ignored him. He went on hurriedly, lifting the cartons from the cart and dropping them carelessly on the ground, not minding even the rattling noise of the bottles in them. But there were only a few cartons left in the cart when Uzo heard the sudden shouts of people in the crowd. Feeling a bit worried, he turned around to see what was happening, but he was too late because he felt just then the weight of something heavy bash the side of his head. He staggered on his feet, and when he regained his balance, it took him a moment to realize what had happened. Even the throbbing pain that made his head feel like it was going to explode came afterwards; after he had seen Kehinde struggling to get up from the ground and after he had felt the warm blood trickling down the side of his face and soaking up the collar of his shirt. But it was the gaping mouths and the horrified expression on the faces of the people in the crowd that said it most. When he finally saw the young man at a distant, glaring like a ghost, and a blood-stained metal rod in his hand, his brows furrowed with rage. Unable to control himself then, he ran towards the young man with his fists clenched for an attack, but a tumult immediately erupted in the crowd, and the people stepped in to prevent the two from coming to blows with each other. Filled with rage, Uzo took off his shirt and began hurling insults at the young man.

When Ajayi showed up a few minutes later, he squeezed himself through the dense crowd to get to Uzo who stood there towering above everyone else.

"Uzo!" He called. "Aarọ owurọ, ati pe o n ja!" Monday morning, and you are already fighting!

Seeing Ajayi, Uzo gathered himself together and stood straight. He was breathing heavily.

"Nibo ni Kehinde wa?" Where is Kehinde? Ajayi asked, furious.

Uzo pointed in the direction where Kehinde was squatting. He too had his t-shirt in his hand and was using it to dab the bleeding gash that resulted from the blow the young man had dealt him with the metal rod.

"Kini o ti ṣẹlẹ?" What happened? Ajayi asked, now more worried than angry.

Still breathing heavily, Uzo pointed at the young man and explained what had happened. Ajayi listened carefully. He thought Uzo and Kehinde should have handled the situation a bit differently, but he knew now was not the time to exchange words with the young man.

"Fi i silẹ, jẹ ki o lọ." Let him go. Ajayi told Uzo. "But warn am well O. Tell am make him no try dis nonsense again."

Uzo was hesitant, but he eventually did as Ajayi instructed. He told the young man to load his cart and get the hell out, and to never sneak into the park again. The young man thanked Ajayi and set about stacking the cartons back onto the cart, and a sigh of relief spread through the crowd. But the crowd had barely dissolved when the young man let out a disturbing cry that drew everyone's attention back to him.

Now, the young man was frantic as he jumped about with his arms wrapped around his head.

"Ah, person go die here O! Ẹnikan yoo ku!" Someone is going to die! The young man threatened at the top of his lungs. He was screaming so loud that the muscles in his temples and neck tightened and his veins became visible. There was a confused feeling in the air as the people watched him jump and scream. Some thought the young man had finally lost his mind. Feeling concerned, an old man with a kufi hat on his head approached him.

"Sannu, abi dey never tell you make you carry your load dey go? Wetin come do you again na?" The man with the kufi hat asked.

The young man threw his hands into the air and grieved. "Ah, Ọlọrun ran mi lọwọ! Dem don carry am!" God help me! They have taken it! He said to the man with the Kufi hat.

"Dem carry wetin?" The man with the kufi hat asked, feeling confused.

"Awọn àpótí! Wọn ti ji diẹ ninu awọn apoti naa!" The cartons! They've stolen some of it! The young man replied.

"Ah-ah!" The man with the kufi hat exclaimed, feeling a bit upset. He looked around worriedly until his eyes caught Uzo and Kehinde walking away with Ajayi in the lead.

"Barayi! Olè!" Thieves! Thieves! The man with the kufi hat screamed as he pointed at the three men. "Catch dem! Make dem no comot!" He added.

The crowd immediately became wild on hearing that loathsome word Olè. That word that everyone at the motor park all agreed was a sin and an abomination that could only be resolved through death and purgation. They acted quickly. Some men seized Uzo and Kehinde, and dragged them back to the place where the young man stood with his half-filled cart. The young man was still screaming.

"Na sixty-four cartons I carry come!" He shouted as he explained his predicament to everyone. "See am na." He said, pulling out a slip of paper he had tucked in-between his waistline and briefs. The man with the kufi hat took the paper from him and examined it. He was right. The paper was a delivery note for sixty-four cartons of wines to a man called Chief Ndubuisi. In a bid to clarify what was written on the paper and his sudden misfortune, the young man explained that he was hired to transport the cartons from the Chief's warehouse to the Chief's shop at the motor park. Everything had been going well until he met these two men, he said pointing to Uzo and Kehinde. The man with the kufi hat nodded to show he understood. But he wanted the young man to recount the cartons to the hearing of everyone so that they could confirm that there were, indeed, some cartons missing. The young man did so and counted only sixty-two cartons. When the crowd heard this, they broke into a loud murmur and everyone turned their attention to Uzo and Kehinde. The two were perplexed, but before they could explain themselves, a group of men set upon them.

The men used their hands and anything they could grab to whack Uzo and Kehinde. Planks, metal rods and pipes landed indiscriminately on the bodies of the two men, tearing their skins open and letting out bright red blood. Meanwhile, Ajayi, who had been protesting since they captured his friends, was growing restless. He could recognize some of the men in the crowd. They were members of a rival gang whose leader often challenged Mama Oshodi's right to control certain territories at the motor park. He swore that one of them had deliberately stolen the cartons so that they could incriminate Uzo and Kehinde, whom they knew very well to be Mama Oshodi's men. They were calling for war, and war they would surely get. But for now, he knew better than to interfere with an angry crowd, especially in a situation such as this one. Fidgeting, he took out his mobile phone and dialled Mama Oshodi's number.

The men were acting fast, and there was nothing Ajayi could do to stop them except run around and pray for Mama Oshodi to show up soon. When he came across some women and children chanting "O-lè! O-lè!" Thieves! Thieves! at the top of their voices, he shushed them, screaming "Apànìyàn!" Murderers! "Ṣe o fẹ lati pa awọn ọkunrin alaiṣẹ!" Do you want to kill innocent men! But the women and children ignored him and carried on with their chants. Then, when he saw two men pull out tyres from underneath a damaged Danfo bus, he felt a cold chill that made the goosebumps on his arms rise. He had witnessed this punishment several times at the motor park, and he knew how it would end. The men threw the tyres around Uzo and Kehinde's heads, and the tyres fell and settled on their shoulders like a big round necklace. Their faces and chests were covered in blood, and they could barely stand on their feet. Kehinde, who had suffered the most beating, held his right arm in an awkward angle. Knowing what the men were about to do, Kehinde made an attempt to stand and escape, but one of the men whacked his head with a wooden plank, and he fell back on his buttocks. Then, they poured petrol on him and ignited the tyre around his neck with a matchstick. Too weak then to put up a fight, he succumbed to the painful stings of burning flames and the terrible fate that had come upon him like a thief in the night.

Meanwhile, Uzo wept and begged. He was desperate for Ajayi and his gang members to come to his aid, but whenever he looked around, all he saw was a crowd that brimmed with strange and angry faces yelling for the men to kill him and save their neighbourhood. The men were just about to empty a petrol can on him when the man with the kufi hat raised his hand to stop them.

"Walahi, na de last time I go ask you dis question." The man with the kufi hat said. "Where you keep dose two cartons?"

"Abeg, I no carry any carton comot for here." Uzo answered, weeping profusely. "Na dis place all of us dey since morning. How I go carry carton?"

"Shut up!" One of the men replied Uzo as he whacked his head a wooden plank. "You no get conscience for your heart!"

Uzo fell to the ground and writhed in pain.

"You talk say you no carry carton, but all of us see you as you dey harass dis man." The man with the kufi hat said, pointing at the young man who owned the cart. He then called the young man forward so that he could reaffirm his statement, but when the young man began to speak, the sound of his ringtone interrupted him. Reaching into his pocket, the young man pulled out his mobile phone and excused himself.

"Ah, ello! Oga mi!" The young man answered, shouting at the top of his voice. It was the chief calling to know why he had not delivered the cartons yet.

"Ah, Oga, big problem dey O!" The young man said to the chief. He told the chief about his experience and the situation he was in, and then at the chief's request, described his location too. When the phone hung up, the young man returned to man with the kufi had and said.

"Abeg, make una wait small. My Oga don dey come."

Now, the pride and arrogance that sustained Uzo's bold and reckless image had fled from him, and his ego had shrunk to the size of an apple seed. He could not believe that the burnt and shrivelled thing next to him was his best friend because it looked nothing more than a Christmas goat on a spit. He thought about home and his parents, and he wished he had hugged his mother goodbye while leaving the house that morning. He thought about his life and how meaningless it seemed, and it pained him that he had not embraced love in his struggle to break free. Then it dawned on him, what made him different from his father. His father had love in his heart but lacked strength, whereas he had strength in his heart but lacked love. He wept.

He was lost in his thoughts when a commotion suddenly broke out in the crowd. People were chanting and screaming a familiar name, and the men that had mobbed him and Kehinde were starting to withdraw. Only the man with the kufi hat stayed back. Uzo narrowed his eyes and looked in the direction of the noise, and when his eyes caught her in the crowd, he felt his heart beat again. She was donning her usual attire: an oversized shirt, loose-fitting jeans, a jaded white pair of trainers and a gold chain around her neck. Behind her, he saw Ajayi and about fifteen men, all armed with machetes and wooden planks. There was a terrible frown on her face when she arrived at the scene, and seeing what remained of Kehinde, she took out a red bandana scarf from her pocket and wiped away tears from her eyes. She wished she had come earlier, and as she stood there looking at the corpse, she fought hard to supress the anger that boiled inside of her. She thought of retaliating immediately, but she knew doing so would only make matters worse. She and her men would suffer more casualties because they were not prepared. Her enemies had caught her by surprise, but she knew just how to get them back. She will wait and strike when the time is right, and when she does, her axe will fall on their head. Her main goal now was to get Uzo out of there.

Ajayi introduced her to the young man who owned the cart and the man with the kufi hat. The young man narrated his encounter with Uzo and Kehinde, and the man with the kufi hat explained why he believed the two were responsible for the missing cartons. But Mama Oshodi dismissed the accusation. She told them that her men would never steal, and that they were only doing their job, which benefited everyone at the motor park.

"No be dese boys wey carry your carton. If you exercise small patience, I promise I go help you find de person wey carry am." She said to the young man. Then turning to the man with the kufi hat, she said to him "As for you, jus make sure you dey always watch your back for dis area. You know as you don spill blood, sometin suppose to follow." And with those statements, she concluded her discussion with the men and ordered Uzo to get up and follow her. Meanwhile, Dada and Tunde, who had been standing next to her looking downcast, moved forward and lifted Kehinde's corpse onto their shoulders. They planned to carry it all the way home to his mother and help her prepare for a proper burial. But Mama Oshodi and her men had barely left the vicinity when the chief arrived with the police. He was a chubby man with a bushy mustache, and he wore a nice looking Ankara dress. There was a sullen look on his face, and he walked with quick steps, like a man on a mission. Following close behind him was a younger-looking man and three police officers. The chief walked up to the young man who owned the cart and ordered him to point out the men with his cartons. Scared and confused, he pointed in the direction of Mama Oshodi and her men.

THE
END

Printed in Great Britain
by Amazon